Amelia's Dream

Written by Lissette Madera

Illustrated By L. A. Jacobs

Novella INDIE Publishing

ISBN: 978-1-5136-9293-7
Library of Congress Control Number: 2022905053

Published by Candi Young
Novella INDIE Publishing
info@kdimglobal.com

Illustrated by L. A. Jacobs,
lajacobs@jacocreativestudios.com

Edited by Shelley Mascia
shelleymascia07@hotmail.com

Formatted by Latricia C. Bailey
consultlatricia@gmail.com

Bulk ordering may be placed by emailing author at:
authormadera@gmail.com or
Publisher at: info@kdimglobal.com

Acknowledgements

A special thanks to my family, Juana, Alex, Andrew, and Jacob, because they have loved and supported me unconditionally.

To Roxanne Ledda for always believing in me and helping me come out of my shell.

My Bank Street College professors, Michele Ryan, and Peggy McNamara, for your support during my Master's experience.

To my publisher, Candi Young, for making this journey of becoming an author a fun one.

Dedication

This is dedicated to my family and loved ones.

This story was inspired by my 3-year-old daughter, Amelia, and all my preschool students who are taken on new adventures full of learning and discoveries.

May all your dreams come true!

Amelia's Dream

This book belongs to _____

Amelia Madera is an adventurous, loving, and brave three-year-old girl.

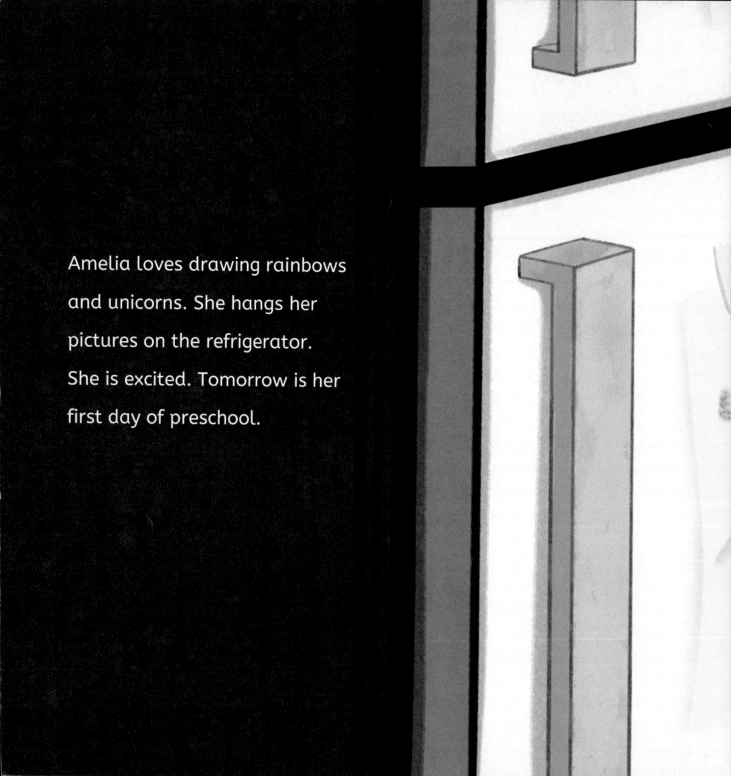

Amelia loves drawing rainbows and unicorns. She hangs her pictures on the refrigerator. She is excited. Tomorrow is her first day of preschool.

After a busy day of coloring, it was time for Amelia to get ready for bed. She said, "*Good night,*" to her two brothers.

Mom and Dad read her favorite bedtime story, tucked her in, and gave Amelia a good night kiss.

Amelia had a hard time falling asleep. She had so many feelings about school the next day. Amelia stared at the stars on her ceiling until she fell asleep.

Suddenly, Amelia was at school. Amelia's mom walked her to her classroom. There was a strange teacher and unfamiliar children. Amelia's tummy grumbled. Her hands were sweaty and her heart was beating fast.

The teacher noticed Amelia was nervous and walked to the door. She greeted her with a kind smile and said, *"Welcome to Garden 3, Amelia! I'm Ms. Juarez and your new classmates are inside. Come in and meet them."*

Amelia's tummy felt better. She wasn't nervous anymore. Amelia walked over to her new classmates but now she felt scared. *"What if they are mean to me?"* she thought.

Ms. Juarez made everyone sit on the rug for circle time. She asked everyone to introduce themselves and share their favorite game. A girl with a fuzzy pink sweater went first.

"Hi, my name is Elizabeth, and I like to play dress up." Amelia became excited! "I like to play dress-up too!" she exclaimed.

Ms. Juarez said, *"That's good to know! Maybe you can play together in our dramatic play area during center time."* Ms. Juarez pointed to an area with toys and a clothing rack.

Amelia listened to her other classmates introduce themselves, but she was impatient. She couldn't wait to play dress-up with Elizabeth! Finally, Ms. Juarez walked Amelia and Elizabeth over to the dramatic play area.

There were so many marvelous toys! There were baby dolls, a cash register, pretend food, and even a real phone! The clothing rack had many different costumes. There was a pretty dress with sequins, a princess gown, a doctor's coat, and even an astronaut suit!

Amelia's eyes lit up when she saw a sparkly tutu. But when Elizabeth saw the same tutu, she wanted it too.

Amelia became angry when Elizabeth reached for the tutu.

"I had it first! It's mine!" Elizabeth said with tears in her eyes.

Ms. Juarez walked over to them and asked them what was wrong.

"She's trying to take my tutu," Amelia cried.

"This tutu is for everyone. I know you're angry right now, but it isn't nice to yell at your friends. It's best to share!" said Ms. Juarez.

Amelia wasn't happy she hurt Elizabeth's feelings.

"I'm sorry I yelled at you. We can share the tutu. Do you want to play with it first?"

Elizabeth smiled and nodded. They had a blast playing together and taking turns. The class was filled with laughter and joy.

Morning came, and Amelia woke up to her mother's voice, *"It's time to wake up, big girl. You have an exciting day ahead of you!"*

Amelia had a big grin on her face. She was ready to take on preschool!

When Amelia arrived at her new school, she wasn't worried! She was excited to make friends. She waited patiently for everyone to arrive.

Amelia's face lit up when she spotted a girl wearing a pink fuzzy sweater walking into the classroom! She didn't look like her friend Elizabeth from her dream, but that didn't matter. Amelia couldn't wait to play and share with her new friends!

The End

Made in the USA
Middletown, DE
10 May 2022

65587981R00020